The Tiara Club

at Ruby Mansions

For ALL the hard working princesses at
Hachette Children's Books,
with love and thanks
VF

www.tiaraclub.co.uk

ORCHARD BOOKS
338 Euston Road, London NW1 3BH
Orchard Books Australia
Level 17/207 Kent St, Sydney NSW 2000

A Paperback Original
First published in Great Britain in 2007
Text © Vivian French 2007
Cover illustration © Sarah Gibb 2007
Inside illustrations © Orchard Books 2007

A CIP catalogue record for this book is available
from the British Library.

ISBN 978 1 84616 293 0

1 3 5 7 9 10 8 6 4 2

Orchard Books is a division of Hachette Children's Books

www.orchardbooks.co.uk

The Tiara Club
at Ruby Mansions

Princess Olivia
and the Velvet Cloak

By Vivian French

ORCHARD BOOKS

The Royal Palace Academy
for the Preparation of Perfect Princesses

(Known to our students as "*The Princess Academy*")

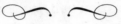

OUR SCHOOL MOTTO:
*A Perfect Princess always thinks of others
before herself, and is kind, caring and truthful.*

Ruby Mansions offers a complete education for Tiara Club princesses with emphasis on the creative arts. The curriculum includes:

*Innovative Ideas for our
Friendship Festival*

*Ballet for Grace
and Poise*

*Designing Floral
Bouquets
(all thorns will be
removed)*

*A visit to the Diamond
Exhibition
(on the joyous occasion of
Queen Fabiola's birthday)*

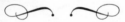

Our headteacher, Queen Fabiola, is present at all times, and students are well looked after by the head fairy godmother, Fairy G, and her assistant, Fairy Angora.

Our resident staff and visiting experts include:

*KING BERNARDO IV
(Ruby Mansions Governor)*

*LADY HARRIS
(Secretary to Queen Fabiola)*

*LADY ARAMINTA
(Princess Academy Matron)*

*QUEEN MOTHER MATILDA
(Etiquette, Posture and
Flower Arranging)*

We award tiara points to encourage our Tiara Club princesses towards the next level. All princesses who win enough points at Ruby Mansions will attend a celebration ball, where they will be presented with their Ruby Sashes.

Ruby Sash Tiara Club princesses are invited to go on to Pearl Palace, our very special residence for Perfect Princesses, where they may continue their education at a higher level.

PLEASE NOTE:
Princesses are expected to arrive at
the Academy with a *minimum* of:

TWENTY BALLGOWNS
(with all necessary hoops,
petticoats, etc)

DANCING SHOES
five pairs

TWELVE DAY DRESSES

VELVET SLIPPERS
three pairs

SEVEN GOWNS
suitable for garden parties,
and other special
day occasions

RIDING BOOTS
two pairs

Cloaks, muffs, stoles, gloves
and other essential
accessories as required

TWELVE TIARAS

Hello! I'm Princess Olivia,
one of the Poppy Room Princesses,
and I'm so pleased you're here too.
Maybe you know Chloe, Jessica, Georgia,
Lauren and Amy? They're my best
friends, and they're LOVELY! Not like
at all like the twins, Diamonde and
Gruella. I know Perfect Princesses
shouldn't be mean about other
princesses, but those two
are SO horrid.

Chapter One

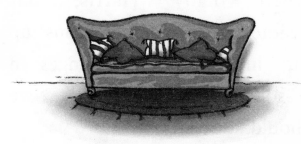

"Nothing exciting EVER seems to happen any more," Jessica said gloomily. "We haven't had any balls or parties for AGES."

We were slumped on the sofas in the recreation room, and it was true. It did feel as if school was going on and ON, and every day was exactly the same.

"Shall I go and look at the noticeboard?" I asked. That's where Lady Harris, our headteacher's assistant, pins up any invitations, or changes in lessons, or anything else we should know about.

Lauren yawned. "I looked on the way down here," she said. "The only new notice is about wearing sensible clothes. We've got to make sure we wrap up warmly when we go outside, because it's getting so cold."

"Do you think it'll snow soon?" Amy asked hopefully. "That would be fun."

I went to look out of the window. "It does look quite cloudy—" I began, and then I stopped. Something VERY strange was happening in the courtyard outside. "QUICK!" I gasped. "Look at THIS!"

My friends flew to join me at the window, and we stared out at the Ruby Mansions footmen hurrying this way and that carrying long planks of wood.

"Whatever are they building?" Chloe's eyes were wide.

"I think it's a stage," Jessica said thoughtfully.

Georgia clapped her hands. "Something exciting MUST be going to happen! What do you think it'll be?"

"Maybe it'll be some kind of play?" I suggested, and I did so hope I was right. I absolutely LOVE acting!

The door to the recreation room opened, and the horrible twins, Diamonde and Gruella, came sweeping in.

"Oooooh!" Diamonde trilled. "Look at the poor little Poppy Roomers peering out of the window! They can't have heard about the Grand Demonstration tomorrow!"

Gruella sniffed. "WE know all about it, don't we, Diamonde?"

"Of course." Diamonde gave us a snooty look. "King Rudolfo is SUCH a good friend of Mummy's, so we know exactly what he's going to do. He's going to show us how Perfect Princesses should behave when a prince lays his cloak on the ground in front of them."

"Why would a prince do that?" Amy asked in surprise.

Gruella rolled her eyes. "REALLY!" she said. "Some princesses don't seem to know ANYTHING, do they, Diamonde? Shall we tell her?"

Diamonde shook her head. "Certainly not. If Amy doesn't know something as simple as that she shouldn't be here." And she stuck her nose in the air and flounced out of the room. Gruella hurried after her.

Jessica made a face as they slammed the door behind them. "They'll be absolutely AWFUL tomorrow," she said. "Bet they show off non-stop."

Amy was still looking puzzled. "Please – somebody tell me about this cloak business!"

"It's a kind of traditional thing," Lauren explained. "If a Perfect Prince sees a Perfect Princess about to get her feet dirty, he's supposed to lay his cloak down on the ground so she can step on that instead."

Georgia smiled at Amy's astonished face. "Silly, isn't it?'

"And actually the cloak makes it worse," Chloe said. "Soggy velvet is EVER so hard to walk across.

I expect that's why we're having a demonstration."

"Do you think we'll get to take turns?" Jessica asked.

"Oh YES!" I said. "That would be such FUN!" And this wonderful picture popped into my head of me floating across a crimson velvet cloak, while a handsome prince bowed low in admiration.

Chapter Two

We were up bright and early the next morning, and we rushed down the stairs to breakfast so fast that Lady Harris, who was standing by the noticeboard, told us off.

"Perfect Princesses do NOT jump the last three steps," she said firmly. "Kindly go back to the first landing, and come down PROPERLY!"

"We're so sorry, Lady Harris," Chloe said politely, and we trooped away back up the stairs to try again. This time Lady Harris allowed us into the dining room, and we were just beginning to eat our porridge when Queen Fabiola, our headteacher, came marching in.

"Princesses!" she said loudly, and waved her ear trumpet at us. "You have SUCH a treat today! King Rudolfo is arriving this morning—"

"See? We TOLD you!" Diamonde hissed in my ear.

"And there will be a Grand Demonstration of Accepting Help with Grace and Elegance," Queen Fabiola went on.

Diamonde and Gruella folded their arms, and gave us an *I-told you-so!* stare, but they sat up VERY straight when Queen Fabiola added, "And King Rudolfo will be bringing a group of princes from the Princes' Academy to help."

It was SO funny! As soon as Queen Fabiola mentioned the princes Diamonde and Gruella began to smooth their hair, and straighten their dresses.

"Just LOOK at Diamonde!" Jessica whispered. "What IS she doing?"

Lauren gasped. "She's tipped tea down her dress! She did it on PURPOSE!"

While we stared, Diamonde put up her hand. "Excuse me, Your Majesty," she said. "May I be excused? I need to change my dress..."

"WHAT? What's that you say?" Queen Fabiola peered at

Diamonde. "What kind of mess? Oh – you silly girl! You've ruined your dress! Run along and change at once. I expect nothing but the VERY BEST from my princesses, in every way!"

As Diamonde hurried out of the dining hall we Poppy Roomers looked at each other. Georgia began to giggle. "She'll be back in her very best ballgown," she said, and she was absolutely right.

Ten minutes later, as we were filing out of the dining hall, Diamonde came back looking AMAZING in a beautiful pale green silk dress with tiny shoulder straps. It was GORGEOUS – but it did look odd on a cold winter's day.

Gruella glared at her. "How come YOU got to change, and I didn't?" she asked crossly.

"One has to look one's best for King Rudolfo and the princes," Diamonde said in a silly grown-up voice. "I'm going to say hello to them right now." And she tossed her hair back as she sailed ahead of us down the corridor.

Gruella made a furious growling noise, and stamped after her.

"I wonder if Diamonde's noticed how cold it is?" Lauren said. "She'll freeze and turn bright blue if she doesn't put something over that dress."

And at that moment Fairy G, our school Fairy Godmother, appeared by the door that led out to the courtyard where the stage had been built.

"Princesses!" she boomed in her loudest voice. "It's very cold outside, so please make sure you're dressed properly!" She caught sight of Diamonde making her way to the door in her silk dress, and her eyes widened. "Goodness me, Princess Diamonde! What ARE you wearing?"

Diamonde frowned. "I've made an effort to look nice for King Rudolfo. He's one of Mummy's BEST friends, you know."

Fairy G raised her eyebrows. "If he's one of your mother's friends, he won't want you freezing to death. Go and put on something sensible." And she stood firmly in Diamonde's way. Diamonde saw me watching, and scowled as she stalked back to her room. Fairy G shook her head, and made sure the rest of us pulled on our boots and

wrapped ourselves in our cosy winter cloaks.

"King Rudolfo and the princes have just arrived," she told us. "Take your places in front of the stage. Once the demonstration is over there'll be hot chocolate and

cinnamon toast for everyone."
She paused, and straightened
Lauren's cloak. "I'm sure I don't
need to tell you to be on your
best behaviour, my dears.
Queen Fabiola is very proud of
her princesses, so don't let her
down – especially in front of King
Rudolfo and the princes!"

Chapter Three

I don't know how she did it, but when we came out into the courtyard Diamonde was already sitting in the very front row. She was wearing a long green velvet cloak that I had never seen before, and she did look very pretty. Gruella was beside her in her everyday winter cloak looking grumpy. As we walked over to the chairs and sat down, I couldn't help wondering why the demonstration had to be outside, but I soon found out. Two pages staggered onto the stage carrying buckets of water, followed by two more with buckets of mud.

"Thank you, lads!" King Rudolfo came hurrying to check what they were doing.

"Could you tip those over the middle of the stage, please?"

The pages nodded, and did as they were told.

"Excellent!" King Rudolfo rubbed his hands together, and smiled. "Now, where are my volunteers?"

A long line of princes, looking wonderfully smart in satin coats and knee breeches, came marching out. Each of them was wearing a crimson velvet cloak and a wide-brimmed hat, and as

they came towards us they
swept off their hats and bowed.
We tried to curtsey back.
I wobbled a bit because I was very
nervous – but Diamonde and
Gruella sank into the deepest
curtsies ever.

"Welcome to Ruby Mansions," Diamonde said in a sugary-sweet voice, and I could tell she was fluttering her eyelashes madly.

The tallest prince, who was VERY handsome, gave Diamonde a dazzling smile.

"May I have the pleasure of asking you to be my partner in the demonstration?" he asked.

"Oh, of COURSE," Diamonde said, and as she stood up she gave Gruella a triumphant smile.

King Rudolfo nodded approvingly. "Princess Diamonde, if I'm not mistaken? I know your mother, my dear."

Diamonde simpered, and bobbed a curtsey.

But King Rudolfo had already turned to the other princes. "Come along," he said. "Invite some of these other delightful princesses to help you."

The princes shuffled their feet and looked embarrassed, but at last they moved forward. A red-haired prince with bright blue eyes came to stand beside me.

"Please," he said, "please will you be my partner?"

"Thank you, Your Highness – I'd be delighted," I said, and I walked with him towards the stage.

As I passed Gruella I heard her hiss, "That's SO not fair! He should have chosen ME!" And she glared at me. I tried to ignore her, but I couldn't help seeing Diamonde giving her sister a sly little wink as I walked up the steps to join the others on the stage.

And I saw something else as well. Diamonde was wearing her sparkly party shoes instead of her boots. I wondered if Fairy G had noticed.

"Time for the demonstration!" King Rudolfo said. "We'll begin with Prince Ferdinand. Prince Ferdinand – please remember everything I've taught you!"

And I suddenly realised that Prince Ferdinand was MY partner, and I hadn't the least idea what to do!

I swallowed hard. It couldn't be that difficult, I told myself. Prince Ferdinand would lay his cloak down over the muddy mess in the middle of the stage, and I would sail across to the other side...and that would be that. He wasn't quite as handsome as the prince I'd imagined, but he did look very nice. I looked at him hopefully, and waited for him to say something.

Nothing happened.

He opened and shut his mouth a couple of times, but no words came out. I tried to smile encouragingly, but that seemed to make him worse. He blushed BRIGHT red, and mopped his face with a corner of his cloak.

King Rudolfo made a tutting noise. "Dear me," he said. "Perhaps we'd better ask Prince George instead."

The prince next to Diamonde bowed, and she looked SO pleased. "Thank you, dear King Rudy," she said. "We'll do our best."

Diamonde stepped forward, and as she passed me she gave me a sharp push with her elbow. I completely lost my balance – and before I knew what was happening I was sliding across the mud in the middle of the stage!

Chapter Four

I don't know HOW I didn't fall over. My arms flailed in all directions and I swayed this way and that way – but I finally reached the other side and staggered onto the bare boards. I must have looked about as unprincessy as it's possible to look, and I heard Diamonde and

Gruella sniggering – but at least I wasn't covered in mud. King Rudolfo was MUCH too polite to laugh, but I could tell nearly all the princes were trying really hard not to giggle. Prince Ferdinand was the only one who looked shocked instead of amused.

I turned, and made my best curtsey to King Rudolfo. "Please excuse me, Your Majesty," I said. "I'm so very sorry...I slipped."

"Princess Olivia! WHAT do you think you're doing?" It was Queen Fabiola, and she was waving her ear trumpet in the air as she stormed her way towards me.

My knees began to tremble. She
sounded furious!

"I came to see how my princesses were enjoying the demonstration, and I find you spinning about in the middle of the stage like a circus clown! What have you to say for yourself?"

I stared down at the wooden boards, and wished I could sink into them. I couldn't explain that Diamonde had pushed me without being a terrible telltale, so I whispered, "If you please, Your Majesty – I lost my balance..."

"I can't hear you, child. You're muttering dreadfully. But such RIDICULOUS behaviour! I'm ashamed of you!" Queen Fabiola looked like a thundercloud. "Go and wait outside my study. I shall speak to you later."

I could feel my face burning as I hurried off the stage and I almost ran back into Ruby Mansions. Behind me, I could hear Queen Fabiola suggesting that everyone had a brisk walk round the courtyard to get warm before Prince George and Diamonde began the demonstration.

I was afraid I might cry, and I was determined not to. That would REALLY make Diamonde happy. I sniffed hard as I walked along the empty corridor, and wondered what was going to happen to me. Would I be given hundreds of minus tiara points...

or would it be something even worse? I stood outside Queen Fabiola's door, and fished in my pocket...

Then someone coughed behind me, and a hand passed me a snow-white hankie.

I spun round – and my mouth fell wide open as I stared and stared. I must have looked like a goldfish, because Prince Ferdinand began to smile.

"What are you doing here?" I asked. "I'm in disgrace!"

"It wasn't your fault," he said firmly. "I saw that horrid girl push you. I tried to tell your headteacher, but she wouldn't listen. She waved me to one side, so I thought I'd follow you, and..." he hesitated, "...and I also wanted to say I'm REALLY sorry I was so useless. If I hadn't had such awful stage fright none of this would have happened."

"That's very nice of you," I said. "And it's OK. It really is."

Prince Ferdinand shook his head. "It isn't. Normally I'm one of the best in the class, but I get SO nervous in front of an audience. Especially when it's girls...hey!" He suddenly looked cheerful. "Why don't I show you? I won't be nervous in front of you."

"What?" I couldn't believe what I was hearing. "You mean...show me how to walk across a cloak?"

"Exactly!" Prince Ferdinand bowed deeply, swept off his velvet cloak, and laid it on the floor in front of me. "Dear Princess Olivia, may I have the pleasure of assisting you across this extremely muddy puddle?"

I couldn't help smiling. "Thank you, Your Highness," I said in my very best Perfect Princess voice. "I would be most grateful." And I tiptoed gracefully across the velvet cloak to the other side while Prince Ferdinand waited patiently.

"Brilliant!" He gave me a huge smile. "I knew you'd be a star!"

"Of course she is!" boomed a voice from the other end of the corridor, and there was Fairy G. She came stomping towards us, and Prince Ferdinand looked at her anxiously.

"It's OK," I whispered. "Fairy G is WONDERFUL!'

"I may be wonderful," Fairy G bellowed, "but could you please explain why you have decided to conduct the most EXCELLENT demonstration all by yourselves in a corridor?'

All at once I remembered what had happened, and I hung my head. Prince Ferdinand stood up very straight.

"Unfortunately Princess Olivia nearly slipped over on the stage, Your Fairyness," he said. "She...she waved her arms like a windmill when she was trying to save herself. Her headmistress thought she was showing off, and sent her indoors, but it SO wasn't her fault. She was pushed by another princess – I was standing right beside her when she did it. And Olivia's much too nice to tell tales, so I'm telling you instead."

"I see," Fairy G said, and her eyes began to twinkle. "Well – perhaps we should go back outside, and see how things are going." And she marched the two of us back along the corridor and out into the courtyard...

…and we were just in time to see Diamonde tripping over in her sparkly party shoes. As she fell she grabbed at Prince George, and he slipped as well – and the two of them fell half on the cloak, and half in the mud.

"OH! OH! OH!" Diamonde screamed. "You STUPID boy! You've RUINED my dress!" And as she picked herself up everyone could see her beautiful ballgown was absolutely covered in mud. Diamonde screamed again, and ran off the stage and away into the school, banging the door behind her. Everyone began to talk at once, but Fairy G stepped forward, and held up her wand.

"I think," she boomed, "we'd better start again. Let's go back to the beginning!"

She waved her wand, and tiny golden sparkles flew in every

direction...and all of a sudden Prince Ferdinand and I were back on the stage! We rubbed our eyes, and stared at each other – and then King Rudolfo spoke.

"Time for the demonstration!" he said. "We'll begin with Prince Ferdinand. Prince Ferdinand – please remember everything I've taught you!"

And Prince Ferdinand gave me the most ENORMOUS grin as he stepped forward.

"Dear Princess Olivia, may I have the pleasure of assisting you across this extremely muddy puddle?"

"Thank you, Your Highness," I said. "I would be most grateful." And – guess what? I tiptoed across just as gracefully as I had when we were in the school corridor, and everyone clapped SO loudly!

And from the back of the audience Queen Fabiola waved her ear trumpet triumphantly. "Give Princess Olivia twenty tiara points, Fairy G!" she called.

"Certainly, Your Majesty," Fairy G said, and she gave me a tiny wink...

It was only after I'd gone back to my seat that I realised things weren't EXACTLY the same as they had been. Diamonde was missing...but a couple of moments later she came hurrying out of the school, and slipped quietly into a seat. As she sat down I found myself looking at her feet – and she was wearing her boots, just like the rest of us!

Chapter Five

It was a while before everyone had had a turn on the stage, but as soon as it was over a group of pages brought out massive trays of hot chocolate and cinnamon toast. It was EXACTLY what we needed to warm us up! We were just finishing our last sips of chocolate when King Rudolfo strode back onto the stage, and clapped his hands to get our attention.

"Princes and princesses," he said. "Queen Fabiola and I are delighted with your work, so we have arranged for the Princes' Academy Musicians to join us. As soon as the stage has been swept clean they will take their positions and play for you – and if that doesn't warm you up, nothing will!"

And he was quite right. The musicians began with the bounciest polka you've ever heard – and who do you think was the first to be invited to dance?

Yes! Me!

Prince Ferdinand seized my hand and whirled me across the courtyard, and it was SUCH fun.

"I knew you'd be good at dancing when I saw you whirligigging across the stage

trying not to fall over," he said with a grin. "And I NEVER get stage fright when I'm dancing!"

"Me neither," I said, and we twirled round and round until we were out of breath ...

And as I went to sit down amongst my lovely friends from Poppy Room, I knew I was the luckiest princess in the whole wide world.

And I'm lucky in another way too – because you're my very special friend!

What happens next?
Find out in

Princess Lauren
and the Diamond Necklace

Greetings, dear princess!
I'm Lauren, by the way. And did
you know I'm a Poppy Room Princess?
Chloe, Jessica, Georgia, Olivia
and Amy are my very best friends, just
like you – and I'm so glad we're all at
Ruby Mansions together. Do you have
day trips in your school? We do, and
we have SUCH fun – just as long as
Diamonde and Gruella don't spoil
everything. You've met them, I'm sure.
They're the horrible twins...

Win a Tiara Club
Perfect Princess Prize!

Look for the secret word in mirror writing that is hidden in a tiara in each of the Tiara Club books. Each book has one word. Put together the six words from books **13** to **18** to make a special Perfect Princess sentence, then send it to us together with 20 words or more on why you like the Tiara Club books. Each month, we will put the correct entries in a draw and one lucky reader will receive a magical Perfect Princess prize!

Send your Perfect Princess sentence,
at least 20 words on why you like the Tiara Club,
your name and your address on a postcard to:
THE TIARA CLUB COMPETITION,
Orchard Books, 338 Euston Road,
London, NW1 3BH

Australian readers should write to:
Hachette Children's Books,
Level 17/207 Kent Street, Sydney, NSW 2000.

Only one entry per child.
Final draw: 31 May 2008

Look out for

Butterfly Ball

with Princess Amy and Princess Olivia!
ISBN 978 1 84616 470 5

*And look out for the Lily Room princesses in
the Tiara Club at Pearl Palace:*

Princess Hannah and the Little Black Kitten
Princess Isabella and the Snow-White Swan
Princess Lucy and the Precious Puppy
Princess Grace and the Golden Nightingale
Princess Ellie and the Enchanted Fawn
Princess Sarah and the Silver Swan

By Vivian French
Illustrated by Sarah Gibb

The Tiara Club

The Tiara Club at Silver Towers

The Tiara Club at Ruby Mansions

PRINCESS CHLOE		
AND THE **PRIMROSE PETTICOATS**	ISBN	978 1 84616 290 9
PRINCESS JESSICA		
AND THE **BEST-FRIEND BRACELET**	ISBN	978 I 84616 291 6
PRINCESS GEORGIA		
AND THE **SHIMMERING PEARL**	ISBN	978 1 84616 292 3
PRINCESS OLIVIA		
AND THE **VELVET CLOAK**	ISBN	978 1 84616 293 0
PRINCESS LAUREN		
AND THE **DIAMOND NECKLACE**	ISBN	978 1 84616 294 7
PRINCESS AMY		
AND THE **GOLDEN COACH**	ISBN	978 1 84616 295 4
CHRISTMAS WONDERLAND	ISBN	978 1 84616 296 1
BUTTERFLY BALL	ISBN	978 1 84616 470 5

All priced at £3.99.
Christmas Wonderland and *Butterfly Ball* are priced at £5.99.
The Tiara Club books are available from all good bookshops, or can be ordered direct
from the publisher: Orchard Books, PO BOX 29, Douglas IM99 IBQ.
Credit card orders please telephone 01624 836000 or fax 01624 837033 or visit our
website: www.wattspub.co.uk or e-mail: bookshop@enterprise.net for details.

To order please quote title, author, ISBN and your full name and address.
Cheques and postal orders should be made payable to 'Bookpost plc.'
Postage and packing is FREE within the UK
(overseas customers should add £2.00 per book).

Prices and availability are subject to change.

Check out

website at:

www.tiaraclub.co.uk

You'll find Perfect Princess games and fun things to do, as well as news on the Tiara Club and all your favourite princesses!